The Adventures of Patrick

How A Pony Became Mayor

By Kirk & Hannah Petrakis

MAPLE
PUBLISHERS

How A Pony Became Mayor

Authors: Kirk & Hannah Petrakis

Copyright © 2023 Kirk & Hannah Petrakis

The authors have asserted the right of Kirk & Hannah Petrakis to be identified as the authors of this work by sections 77 and 78 of the Copyright, Designs and Patents Act 1988.

First Published in 2023

ISBN 978-1-915996-35-0 (Paperback)
     978-1-915996-36-7 (Hardback)
     978-1-915996-37-4 (E-Book)

Book cover design, Illustrations and Book layout by:
     White Magic Studios
     www.whitemagicstudios.co.uk

Published by:
     Maple Publishers
     Fairbourne Drive, Atterbury,
     Milton Keynes,
     MK10 9RG, UK
     www.maplepublishers.com

Neigh! Hurray! It is a beautiful day. Patrick, the pony, wakes up to Joe Robin who is plucking out his moulting coat, which is shedding in the spring air. The birds are grateful for the pony hair, which they use in their nest, as it makes it cosy for them to rest.

Clippity, clop, Patrick, the pony, trots into the village of Cockington — a village with beautiful thatched roofs, and stone-walled cafes, where families are sat at tables under umbrellas enjoying cream teas, sometimes avoiding curious bees.

When they hear those tiny hooves, they turn around to look at a Miniature Shetland Pony enjoying his walk. Many grab their devices to take a photo, as he is just so cute. They want to show their friends, the pony they got to stroke.

The red bus pulls up and invites Patrick on. He is delighted to be driven along. They went through the narrow Devon country lanes, with hedges so high, he couldn't see what was behind.

A voice shouted out, "Stop, stop, you can't have a pony on a bus." It was Mr Ghastly, who was often very nasty.

The driver said, "Everyone is welcome to travel, here in Devon."

Patrick went to the Post Office. They needed his help delivering some letters, as the Postman was ill.

Mr Ghastly shouted out, "You can't have a pony in the shop, get him out."

Mrs Red said, "Everyone is welcome in our shop. Patrick is helping me today, so please be kind or go on your way."

Once the last letter was delivered, Mrs Red said, "Patrick, you are so clever. Thank you, now I feel much better. You are so helpful to everyone. I hope someday you will be the Mayor as you always show everyone how much you care."

The Park Ranger, Mr Green, was repairing the bridge. He couldn't use his truck as there was too much mud, so Patrick offered to help. He was very strong and was able to pull the planks of wood along.

Mr Ghastly shouted, "You can't associate with that pony, he smells. Crack on, Mr Green, and do it all, yourself."

Mr Green was not very pleased. He said, "Patrick, the pony, is my friend, he is helping me today. Please be kind or be on your way."

Together they rebuilt the bridge, which allowed all the people and animals to get to the village.

An old lady was looking sad as she was struggling with many bags.

Patrick came trotting with a trolley, so she could put the shopping in. He helped her home, and she was happy she was not alone.

She said, "Thank you, kind Patrick, here is a carrot before you go on your way."

Patrick goes to the red phone box to call his friends all over the world, to let them know how much he loves them.

There was a smell of smoke. It made Patrick feel like he was going to choke. A thatch roof was on fire, he called for help. The red fire engine was quick, it arrived just in time, they were able to put it out.

Mr Peg's home was saved and thankfully no one got hurt. He said, "Thank you, Patrick, for calling for help, you really did save the day."

Patrick replied with a neigh.

Poor Lucy Red let out a scream, as she had got trapped in the shed. The door had become stuck in a wedge. Patrick was quick, he gave out a kick, which caused the door to open with a click. She came running out and gave Patrick a pat on the head.

All the residents received an important letter inviting them to a village meeting, to discuss the idea of electing a new Mayor. They needed to find someone who could always be there and genuinely cared.

Mr Ghastly shouted out, "This should be me, I want to be the Mayor, as I know everything that goes on and I have lived here for so long."

The locals arrived for the meeting, with chairs put out in a circle. Mr Ghastly marches in with a grin and says, "When I become the village Mayor, I will need a fancy red velvet cloak, with a lace collar and a gold chain of honour."

Mr Green said, "Mr Ghastly, you must be having a joke, we all need to vote."

Those who chose to vote, did so in private. Now we must reveal who has been chosen by the people.

Patrick, The Pony's, name is on all the slips, apart from one.

Mr Ghastly shouts out in anger, "This cannot be, I voted for me. Good golly, it cannot be a pony."

Mr Green said, "If you can't be nice, be on your way, as Patrick is now our Mayor, so don't be a sour grape."

The old lady loved to sew, she let everyone know, that she was delighted to create the red rug for a pony Mayor, which needed such care. The design was soft and red, with a white trim and a tie to go under the tail. It was made to measure, as it was such a treasure. A white diamond collar, to sit in between Patrick's shoulders, with lace to highlight his face.

The Blacksmith at the forge - his name was George - banged his hammer on the chain which shaped it, so it could sit comfortably on Patrick's mane. This chain of office was like no other, it had gold lights, so it could be seen even at night. This gold medallion was the envy of every stallion, but Patrick would wear it with only grace, not a trace of arrogance upon his face.

The red steam train came chugging along, which whistled like a mystical song; the locomotives provide the force for it to move along the tracks.

This steam train was delivering a very special red velvet box, for the new pony Mayor - gold boots, there were 4, specially made far away for his little hooves, cushioned for comfort with the most luxurious fabrics, with velcro straps.

It was time for the ceremony, where this cute little pony would be officially appointed the Mayor. He was chosen because he was kind and proved he was always there, as a pony who cared.

Everyone came from all over, even the animals rejoiced with the people's choice.

A man of position presented Patrick, The Pony, with his official chain of office.

His gold shiny boots, looked extremely cute, with a red rug that was hand made for this special day.

Everyone shouted with delight: "Patrick, The Pony, saved the day, now he is the first Miniature Shetland Pony Mayor."

Now it was time to celebrate. Mrs Red had made plenty of cake. The Band arrived just in time, with cheering locals, who were very vocal, as they were excited to sing their favourite song Neigh Hurray!

Neigh, Hurray

Say Hi to Patrick the special pony
He'll cheer you up if you're sad and lonely
Just call for Patrick, he's on his way
And he'll come trotting and save the day.

Scan the Code to access the Song, so you can sing along

Oh Neigh, Hurray, oh Neigh, Hurray
Patrick is coming, he'll save the day.

His name is Patrick he wants to meet you
Just pat his nose now and let him greet you,
His big brown eyes are very friendly,
Don't pull his ears, please, just stroke him gently.

Oh Neigh, Hurray, Oh Neigh,
Hurray,
Patrick is coming, he'll save the day

He's just a pony, a little pony
We like to think he's one and only
Patrick, we love you, you're such a dear,
We are always happy when you are near

Oh Neigh, Hurray, Oh Neigh, Hurray,
Now here comes Patrick he'll save the day,
Oh Neigh, Hurray, Oh Neigh, Hurray,
Three cheers for Patrick, he's saved the day.

Patrick The Pony
Signed hoof print

The actual size of hoof:

2.5 inches across

2.75 inches height

2.5 inches

2.75 inches

Meet the real Patrick

Connect on Facebook

Connect on Instagram

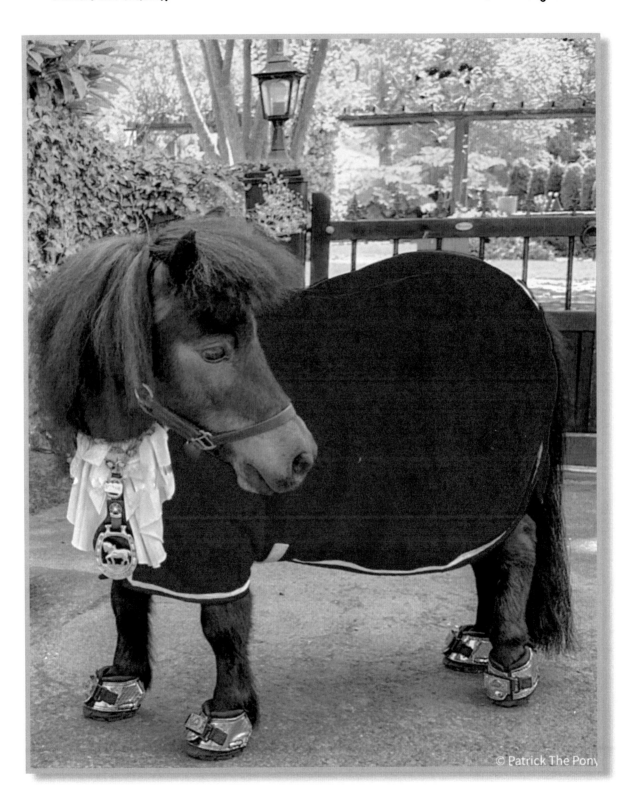

© Patrick The Pony

Made in the USA
Middletown, DE
11 April 2024

52849479R00029